T0366269

TWO

Written By

Jillian M. Capodiferro

Illustrated By

Laura A. Foley

www.trafford.com
North America & international
toll-free: 1 888 232 4444 (USA & Canada)
fax: 812 355 4082

CHARACTERS

Katy Whitman—the girl Ambrosh
is in love with (a human)
Susan—Katy's friend
Peter—Katy's little brother
Jake Hopkins—Katy's friend

Ambrosh—the main vampire

Regimore—vampire hunter

PART 1

CHAPTER 1

Katy Whitman was looking out the window of her room again. Through the beige curtain, she could see twilight. Her room gloomed with serenity. Her company pulled into the driveway. She went to meet them. When she got to the car, they said "Ya ready, Katy?"

"Yeah!" she said.

***

Ambrosh had an awakening in a cave, but the awakening was subtle. They (others) were added to the group of vampires. He went out to hunt every evening. When he breathed, it sounded like hissing.

It was as if a shroud draped about him that shielded him from the wind. He walked in sorrow. When he drank, he felt free! Free of his cares and free of the shroud. But when reality sank in, again he was trapped.

The shroud felt like a damp cover: it inhibited him. He was always thirsty. Only when he drank did the shroud momentarily leave him. When the shroud would momentarily leave him, he felt happy! He was the oldest vampire in existence, about as old as Regimore was.

The vampires took the lives of mortals every night, while the hunters searched for them in the daylight hours. These two men were as different as the times they did their work, day and night—Regimore and Ambrosh.

***

Katy was fixated on the dead that summer. She was a rebel. She would go at night to sit by the water to have peace. Katy Whitman lived in Pesdonia.

***

The hunters knew of the vampires. They knew of their ways, of their methods, of their marks. They knew of the living dead. The corpses' disappearances from the morgue every night were because of them. Regimore worked in the morgue too. That was his second job. He didn't live in the village. He was also a watchmaker in the city. He spent most of his time in the back room, creating a number of watches. He was a big, robust man who spoke softly yet surely.

Katy sometimes spoke with him. Regimore thought it was a very dangerous thing that Katy did.

***

At night, a shadow would throw itself upon this town. Pesdonia would use its streetlights for light at night. The inhabitants of the town would be exhausted. They would sleep, unaware of the night breed. Everyone slept, except for Regimore, Katy, and Ambrosh.

Slowly their eyes would roll open, as slower still they would revive. They would all arise at once; they moved swiftly, like cats. They were true children of the night—the vampires.

***

One night, Ambrosh went to the docks and saw Katy there. He spared her then. He looked at her through the reeds and tall grass.

He was caught! The one glimpse of her got him hooked, and he wanted more. It was like he saw a leaf and wanted the whole forest. He felt free and alive. The shroud, for that moment, felt like it had fallen off him. He didn't regret that he had nothing to drink in the morning.

It was as if looking at her released a swan; however temporary, it was beautiful. He would have loved for this feeling to stay; it would have filled him with joy. Yet time was limited, and soon dawn would come. Back to the cave, the shroud, the dirt.

He wanted to sit beside her, to sit adjacent to his other swan.

He had to run "home." He felt compelled to vanish. He extended each leg further from the ground until they lifted up and kicked into a run.

He made it back before the sun came up.

He would have liked to see her again. Yet he had to eat/ drink.

He chose his prey carefully.

First, he lingered behind their steps, stalking them. Then he swiftly overtook them as they were unaware. He gripped their necks and sank his teeth into his victim's flesh. It sounded like paper being crumpled. He indulged plentifully. In the process of drinking, he felt like he was traveling through their bloodstream.

Blood gathered in the center of his lower lip and dripped slowly. Then he let go of the lifeless victim. The moon above glistened. He traveled onward from raw instinct to the next. The cloak charged him a plentiful price, and he would be forever in its debt.

CHAPTER 2

"You're working on one of these today? I knew you would be." Katy said.

Regimore replied, "Yes, one of those. Been working until late these past few nights?"

Katy was silent.

"I have to go, Regimore." And she left. She was distant.

It was still light when she got back to her home. She had to get ready to leave, and so she went to her room.

✳✳✳

He watched her from his tomb and tried to whisper to her. Yet she was protected, and the wind never carried these words to her ears.

✳✳✳

She traveled through the thickets and twisting paths. She weaved her way through the barren trees. *Come on, legs,* she thought to herself.

She found a clearing and sat down surrounded by tall grass. It was like she was in a trance. She fell back.

"Your winds glide my sails 'cross glittering seas . . ."

She kept thinking.

Ambrosh tried to speak to her.

Then it started to rain, and she went home.

✳✳✳

The sun dried everything up, and Katy was in her room.

She was recalling the night before and the words.

She recalled, "Your winds glide my sails 'cross glittering seas . . ."

And she repeated, "'cross glittering seas . . ."

She stopped suddenly. She got on her bike outside. She got on the bike and rode. She saw the ground beneath her steadily advance under the tire. She rode to Regimores'.

***

He was walking along the beach; the waves were crashing at his side. He saw a small child sitting alone, looking down at the stick in his hand. He stood over him and said, "What ya doing here, little guy?"

The child was about one year old. Regimore placed a hand on the boy's head, and the boy smiled and giggled.

"Donald? Donald?" trailed his mother's voice in the distance.

***

Now Regimore was sitting in front of the shop. He was sitting on a chair. Upon hearing the front door open, he looked up, peering through his glasses, and said, "Katy, what a delight to see you."

"Regimore . . . What is it? What can it be?" Katy was confused.

He said, "Yes, Katy, what can it be?"

Regimore was before her, while the sea was in her mind.

She said, "The sea . . ." She was confused and thinking of her experience.

Pausing after a moment, he said, "Is not the day most appealing, Katy?"

Then he said this, "Katy, just remember this . . . You were not made for the night."

***

Ambrosh returned to his domain. He walked indifferently.

Outside, the sun had risen. It was damp outside. Now everything was vibrantly lit; all traces of night were gone. Those eyes were demanding. They were purring. They wanted Katy.

They wanted her for her purity, longing to corrupt it. Ambrosh was not listening to their pleas. They did not suggest life.

"Silence!" he demanded.

His voice caused their purring to cease.

They were hungry.

"Nothing, there is nothing tonight . . . Nothing!"

They stopped.

Now he exited his chamber. He was thinking of them and of Katy. Then he screamed, and it echoed through the place.

PART 2

CHAPTER 3

Night fell upon the land. She went out again, but she found no delight in her escape. The scene no longer held her attention, and she wanted to leave. Then the wind blew; it kept her there as night fell more fully. The crickets' chirps penetrated the scenery. Hours passed. Everything became silent, then Katy stood up.

Cupping her hands, she called, "Hello?"

It echoed. *Hello? . . . Hello? . . . Hello?*

"Hello, is there . . ."

It was no use.

Katy heard branches breaking and something moving. She sat down again. She did not move.

Another crack, more branches breaking.

She screamed, "Ahh!"

She heard purring. The sound of purring filled the forest. Then there was no more breaking, no more cracking, no more purring. Katy did not move. She calmed down.

Then they popped up—the green eyes, the female vampires. "Katy," one said.

At first, Katy froze, not believing this was happening to her. Then she reached down and frantically picked up a few stones and threw it at them. Then she started to run and didn't stop.

She ran through the forest. She bumped into various trees but didn't care. She sprinted through the forest with great speed. She could feel her heart racing. She ran as fast as she could.

Suddenly, there were lights on the edge of the ravine. She heard voices. So she yelled out, "Is there anybody there?"

"Yes, yes!" she heard. It was the hunters.

She reached the lightened patch of clear earth and fell to the ground.

"Check her neck! Check her neck!" one said.

"We need to test her blood!" another one asserted.

"Isolate her until sunrise!" still a third stated.

"Please allow me to go home," she spoke softly to the hunters after she had caught her breath.

"Who are you? What in God's name are you doing out at this hour? Out at this hour in Pesdonia? Foolish child!" one hunter exclaimed.

"What are we to tell Regimore, tell him that Pesdonia's youth roam the streets in the peak of the breed's search? Same like that other fellow, Jacob Hopkins, I believe," stated another hunter.

"And who was that?" a third hunter asked.

"The boy who was out late the other night. He did not encounter Ambrosh or the others, but still the night was calm," one hunter asserted.

"What breed?" Katy asked, dumbfounded.

"You probably saw one of them tonight. Did the forest purr?" he asked her.

Katy was silent and shocked.

"We'd better bring her home before it gets late. It is obvious she has encountered Tabathia or one of the other mistresses. Why her life was not taken, I do not know, for there is none who can outrun them. She is in shock," one finally stated.

✳✳✳

Katy was home, in her room, recovering. "It was not real It couldn't have been!"

Then she remembered the green eyes and Tabathia's voice saying, "Katy."

She screamed, "Ahh!"

"Katy, Katy, what is it?" Her parents came into the room. They were unbelievers.

"It was nothing, nothing . . ." Then she realized that she could not bury this. "Mom, Mom, her eyes, her mouth," she talked loudly. "She was real! She was real. She was not nothing, she was not!"

The father spoke, "Katherine, go get a cold rag."

"Feel her head, Jon?" said the mother.

"I don't need to feel her head to know it's a fever," exclaimed her dad.

"Katy, you need to sleep now," suggested her mother.

***

Regimore was asking the other hunters, "Did she tell you her name?"

"No, she did not. She was all worked up, could imagine she broke when she got home. She met Tabathia, we are sure of that," the other hunters answered.

"Tabathia . . . Ahh . . ." said Regimore. "Yes, she is the finest of the females."

"Yes, I do know. What I do not know is why she was spared, why she wasn't killed," the other hunter answered.

"The night is a very funny thing. You know you never can predict these things. Do not waste your strength."

"Regimore, that is the second," another hunter reminded Regimore.

"There is a first?" Regimore asked.

"Yes, his name is Jacob Hopkins."

"Very well, very well. Tell me of him. How did you explain yourselves to him?" Regimore asked.

"We explained that we worked for the benefits of this fine city," they stated.

"And his response?" Regimore wanted to know.

His response was "I thought you were here to hunt the vampires!"

"Very well, he will serve his purpose in consoling the girl," Regimore concluded.

***

Nothing was working for Katy's fever. Nothing could suggest to Katy that her encounter was not real.

She went to knock on Jake's door. She knocked.

His father answered.

"Hello, is Jake home? I'm Katy, from his history class. I came to get the assignment from him because I was absent."

He said, "Okay." Then he turned and went to get him.

Jake appeared before her.

"Jake Hopkins?" she asked.

Jake said, "You're not the Katy from my history class!"

Katy said, "No, I'm not. I must ask you something. What happened to you the night you stayed out? And what can you tell me of the vampires?"

"Okay," he said, "we can talk. Let's walk and talk!"

Jacob and Katy talked for hours. They were friends.

"So then I went to the lake . . ." He was in the middle of his story.

"The lake?" she repeated.

"Yeah, why, what's wrong?"

Remembering, Katy said, "That place is significant! There was one time I was there." She told him of that one night.

"But I still like the lake!" she said. "I don't think it will happen again."

"Why not?" asked Jake.

"I think they're fasting, and besides, nothing will happen in the day."

So they would meet at the lake during the day. Only the day.

***

"He never visits us, but instead dreams of that—"

"Katy!" Tabathia answered.

"We cannot hunt unaccompanied by him!" the other female added.

"How many more nights shall pass? Already it has been three since Tabathia's last attempt, and still we are—" the second female said.

"I permitted her to leave me!" Tabathia paused before continuing, "Precious being that she is. Tonight, my beauties, we will eat."

CHAPTER 4

"Katy, look, come here," said Susan.

They were in Susan's garden; it smelled good.

"What is it? Other than those flowers you love?" asked Katy.

"Oh, forget the flowers and come over here and see this," said Susan.

Katy went over there.

"This book I got the other day from the library. As soon as I saw it, I thought of you. It reminded me of the night you had a fever," said Susan gleefully.

"Yeah. Haha! What is it? A book about vampires?" asked Katy.

"Yes!" said Susan.

"Wow!" She took it and flipped through it. "How old is it?" Katy asked. "Thank you, Susan."

Then she called Jacob. "Jacob, you've got to see this. You know what I got today?" She paused. "I've got a book on vampires!" Katy exclaimed.

"A book on what?" he asked.

"Vampires!" she repeated. "You've got to see this! I can't talk now, but you can meet me tonight at the lake."

"Tonight?" he repeated, alarmed.

"Yes, tonight."

"But I thought we agreed—" he began.

"Agreed nothing. We agreed to meet if something important happened. Well, this is important!" she stated.

"Well, if it's okay with you," said Jake, uncertain.

"Yes, be there by nine o'clock sharp."

***

Katy walked down the steps. "What ya watching, Peter?" she asked.

"Awesome, stupid rerun," he answered.

"Perhaps we should call it a night, no?" she said.

He was a toddler and her brother. He yawned, and she ran her hand through his brown hair. "I love you, little!" Katy stated.

"I'm not little!" Peter replied.

She got the keys and left through the glass doors. It was 8:30 p.m.

***

Ambrosh was in front of her house. As soon as she left, he followed.

Ambrosh went to the lake and saw Jake. He went before him and commanded, "Be gone!"

Jake fell to the ground when he said this. His balance was off.

***

Katy drove to the lake. She called out, "Jacob?"

***

Jacob was running through the woods. He ran as fast as he could. He ran straight home. He banged into the door, then closed and locked it. Then he thought, *What about Katy?*

***

He rose from behind a bush. She saw him.

"No," Ambrosh said. "It is not your faithful Jacob."

"Where is he?" she demanded. She looked at him more, then asked, "Who are you?"

"I am Ambrosh!" he answered, adding, "Who are you?"

She was lost. There was some sort of trance that she was in. She remembered Susan saying, "As soon as I saw it, I thought of you." She was in a fog.

Regrouping, she demanded again, "Where is Jacob? Where is he? Where?"

A twig snapped in the distance.

A small voice asked, "Katy?"

"Peter!"

"Katy, I'm scared!"

She ran and picked up her little brother, Peter, who had followed her.

✻✻✻

She was home the next night. She left and went to the lake. She sat down. It was night.

"Katy? Are you crazy?"

She was confused. "Jacob?"

"Oh my God! Here at night? Are you absolutely crazy? Katy, he could be here. Right *here*! We're going home!" he stated.

"Who, Jacob?" Katy asked. "Jacob, what are you talking about?"

"We must leave!" he stated. "There was someone, something here last night. Something awful, we must— I called your mother today. She said that you were out late last night and that Peter followed you and he couldn't stop crying for hours once he got home. I was not there. He wants you! What happened last night?"

She was looking down at him. Then he dropped to the floor. "Jacob!" she almost screamed.

The three were there. She heard purring.

CHAPTER 5

She woke up in a stone chamber. It was dark. She knew she was no longer in the forest. Jacob was not on the floor in front of her. She went to feel around.

Ambrosh was there. He was outside the door. Then he went into his room.

***

"They have taken her away! You know that, don't you? I am unsure who it was, either him or them. She is gone though.

This I am sure of. Permit the boy to leave at night. He is our only hope," the hunter stated.

"Who? Who is this boy?" Regimore asked.

"Jake. Jacob Hopkins," he answered.

***

It was dawn, and he woke up. He lifted himself from the ground. He looked around; he was dazed. Instantly, he was aware they had taken Katy.

But where did they take her? he thought. Where?

Then he knew. *Ocean.*

***

"Jake, Jake?" his mother asked. "Where are you going?"

"To a friend's for the weekend. I'll be back later."

"Later? Jacob?"

"Please." He was absorbed in preparation.

***

She was still in the chamber, in the dark. She pulled up to and looked out the window and saw the ocean. It was night, and the moon shone brightly. The moonlight made something almost like a pathway on the water and shone on her tired face. She accepted the frustration. Then she backed away from the window and tried to get some rest.

Down along the water were the three females holding a body. Katy waited for the morning light as they feasted. Their eyes were glowing green.

***

Jake walked backward on a ditch road, one thumb out, hitchhiking. Then a car came to a stop. He got in.

"Where'd you say you were going?"

"Misty's Point."

"Ain't that a long way on foot?"

"Yeah," Jake answered, getting in.

Once seated, as they were going, he asked, "Can we drive quicker?"

"Come in here and stop shaving," Jake's mom called to her husband.

"One second!" he answered through the bathroom door.

"Okay, I'll push stop," the wife said.

"Where'd you say Jake went again?" he called.

"Over at a friend's for the weekend," his wife answered.

"Oh, okay . . . Where is it?" Jake's father exclaimed loudly. He came out of the bathroom with shaving cream on his face. "By any chance, Hale, have you seen my shaving mirror?"

She was sleeping in the room. Ambrosh was standing outside. He would never be in her dreams; her heart was with Jake. Then she heard a gnawing sound at the door. It was the female vampires. The wood on the door was splintering. Then it stopped.

Tabathia went to Ambrosh's room, holding a body. He no longer went out to hunt, so Tabathia brought him some food.

A mist now covered the ocean. Jake stepped out of the car. The people in the car said, "Well, we sure hope you find whatever you came out here looking for."

He answered, "Yeah, I will. Thanks."

The car drove away. Jake walked toward the estate.

There was a door just before the entrance. It looked like an old gate. It had ivy growing on it. In the daylight it would have been very pretty.

Jake walked past a giant pine. He was small in comparison to that. Water droplets from the ocean brushed against his face. *How am I gonna get in?* he wondered. *The tree!*

He looked at the tall house then stepped by the tree. When he got to it, he began to lift himself up.

She was pacing around her room now, thinking of Jake. *Is he still in the forest, by the lake, alone?* If regret could bring him back, it would, but it can't. Her physical body was pacing, but her spirit was with Jake over the water, in the woods, at the lake.

Jake climbed in through a window. He landed with a thump. The room was dark. Then he exclaimed, "What the heck!"

The corridor lay before him. Ambrosh was at the other end. Although Jake could only see a silhouette, he knew who it was.

Morning had come. Peter gazed out the window sadly. His mother was busy preparing breakfast. When she was finished, she went to the table. She asked, perplexed, "Peter, aren't you hungry?"

Peter looked out the window and asked his mom, "Where is she, Mama?"

The mother put her hands on his back lovingly and answered, "I just don't know, Peter!"

The broadcast from the radio was all muffled.

"Damn static," Jim said. "It's because of the mountains." He was the man Jacob had gotten a ride from. He reached into the other seat. "Oh, looks like our old friend left his mirror behind!" Pulling it out and holding it up, Jim said, "Looks like Jim got himself a new shaving mirror."

Jake opened Katy's door. She ran to him and embraced him. "I hoped it would be you!" she stated.

The hunters stood outside the estate with wooden stakes in their hands. As they stood, a fleeting breeze brushed across their faces and reminded them of the days that were no more!

Printed in the United States
By Bookmasters